# An Explosion of White Petals

an anthology of student poetry
from the Minnesota Poets in the Schools program,
1978-79, COMPAS

edited by Mark Vinz
illustration and design by Gaylord Schanilec

# Acknowledgements

Copyright © 1979 by COMPAS

No part of this book may be reprinted or reproduced without the prior permission of COMPAS.

An agency of the St. Paul-Ramsey Arts and Science Council, COMPAS (Community Programs in the Arts and Sciences), is responsible for conducting a wide variety of arts programs, of which Poets in the Schools is one. Poets in the Schools (next year to include prose writers and playwrights and to be called "Writers in the Schools") helps place professional poets in residence in schools and communities throughout the state.

Support for COMPAS Poets in the Schools' activities comes from the National Endowment for the Arts, the City of St. Paul, local foundations including the Green Giant Company, Northwest Area Foundation, Jerome Foundation and General Mills, Minnesota schools, the Comprehensive Employment and Training Act (CETA) — U.S. Department of Labor, and the Minnesota State Arts Board with funds appropriated from the Minnesota State Legislature.

>For further information, contact:
>Molly LaBerge, Executive Director
>COMPAS
>Landmark Center
>75 W. 5th St.
>St. Paul, MN 55102

Production of *An Explosion of White Petals* by Margaret Hasse, assisted by Julie Leavitt.

# Introductions

This collection of poems represents the work of 23 poets in more than 80 weeks of residencies in schools throughout Minnesota. The poets themselves made the initial selections from among the hundreds, even thousands of poems they received; I simply made the final choices — approximately one poem from each week of residency. My job has been a joyous one.

What I've tried to emphasize in my choices is both variety and surprise. The predominant theme in the poems I read is intensely personal feeling, often painful, almost always frank. This reaffirms for me some of the basic principles of all poetry: to discover and express parts of us that are hidden (sometimes from ourselves), to reach out, and to learn how to find new words, new ways of perceiving both the inner and outer worlds.

Some part of what Poets in the Schools can accomplish should be evident in these pages, though what we are able to begin in the classroom must also be built upon and encouraged. As stated so well in a poem once given to me by a student from Princeton High School, we must never forget to *hear* these voices:

>    That Strange Animal, The Poet
>
>    Poets are strange beings.
>    They talk in proverbs,
>    dwell in metaphors.
>    They see
>    sadness
>    in a smile,
>    and delight in
>    nightmares.
>    But funniest of all,
>    they listen when I talk.
>            — Tammy Sundberg

As a writer, a teacher, and a parent, I must reaffirm my pride in the Minnesota Poets in the Schools Program, and my thanks to those who have administered it so very well. As Margaret Hasse said in the introduction to last year's anthology, such a work is truly a celebration.  That's what all of us have been involved in: a gathering, a celebration, a reaching out.

>Mark Vinz
>editor and writer
>Poets in the Schools

Getting a book through production takes a long time.  This book began in the early spring of 1977 when teachers, community members and administrators in schools chose to budget matching money and apply for a grant to have a poet come to their classrooms.  A commitment was made to arts and education — not only of money, but of time and enthusiasm.  The schools were acknowledging the value of the interaction between writers and other people who wanted to participate together in creating with language.

*An Explosion of White Petals* was actually written by 50,000 people, for that is the number of students, faculty and interested community members who worked with the poets, who read and heard poems, who entered into a process of self-awareness and creative use of language.

Special recognition should go to the poets who worked with the 78-79 program and who were encouraging and concerned teachers as well as artists.  The names of the poets and the schools they visited are listed in the index at the back of the book.

>Margaret Hasse
>Director, 78-79
>Poets in the Schools, COMPAS

# An Explosion of White Petals

## THINGS TO HOLD AND BEAUTIFUL SOUNDS

I hold the secret. It is hard
to hold a secret inside your
body. The light is shining,
the wind is blowing, and me
using words to describe things.
The wind stops the birds come
out and start to sing in the
light. The birds are happily
singing.

*Christina Alvarado/grade 3*
*Roosevelt Elementary, St. Paul*




On the day of the eclipse
in mid-afternoon
I listen for feathers.
I search for dreams.
I climb the sky.
I watch for rivers of silver.
I am lost among treetops.
I begin with Z.
I wear shoes made of mountains
and I sleep through darkness
with teachers at my feet.

*Jill Miller/grade 3*
*Washburn Elementary, Bloomington*

a wind tiger

Did you ever hear of wind tigers?
They fly!
They whistle because the air
goes right through them.
They have holes.
They fly into the windows of
imagination.

*Debby O'Brien/grade 5*
*Silver Oak Elementary, St. Anthony Village*

## AT 75

I sit watching the fireworks go off,
sitting in the middle of my
garden, watching people across the
street lighting fireworks, the faces
of the little ones light up.

On this hot July night I sit here
remembering when I was twenty-one or
two, when my family would get together
and shoot off firecrackers, light
sparklers.

But now I am 74 and growing old. I
am like a firecracker that has already
gone off and is fading in the sky.
Tomorrow I'll be 75.

*Chris Wilcox/grade 5-6*
*Lincoln Elementary, Moorhead*

A PREVIOUS LIFE

Last time I was here was autumn. The deck always gave
me splinters. The breeze smelled of drying pine sap. The
leaves were winding down to the ground. The grey squirrel
that always clicked was gathering more nuts for its long
sleep. Smoke from fires up-wind fills the air with death.
Cool breezes off the lake drift in, bring new life.

*David Roberts/grade 9*
*Edina East High School, Edina*

If you were leaving, I'd give you a book,
   so you could have the knowledge of the world.
I'd give you my eyes to see baby chicks hatching from their shells,
   white as the clouds in the sky.
I'd give you the sun to protect you from darkness.
I'd give you a tree to protect you from rain,
   like tiny stones a child throws into a quiet pond.
I'd give you a rose so you could smell the morning dew
   on the grasses, clear and bright.
I'd give you a pair of wings so you can be free
   like the wind blowing through prairie grasses.
I'd give the earth as a gift of love.
I'd give you anything, dear child, for I am your father.

*Kathy Nordgaard/grade 7*
*North Branch Middle School, North Branch*

## ALIENATION

    The day,
a crumbling farm house
    grey, cold
    empty and
        dark.
    No life
except for an occasional
        car
    passing by
    like a lone mouse
scurrying across the dirty floor.

Wind, damp and chilling.
    I am alone
    peering out the
        broken window
    breeze seeping in through the
        cracks in the
        wood.
A familiar smell —
memories of walking to
    school
    on a rainy
        morning
    seeing dead worms
        lying on the
            road.

*Mary Peterson/grade 12*
*Glencoe High School, Glencoe*

Thursdays are like
   cities of cement, rough and
      hard.
Thursdays are like
   walking the elephant, big
      and bulky.
Thursdays are like
   studying the floor, dull
      and blank.
Thursdays are like a mask of iron,
   keeping you away from
      the other world.

*Blake Wagner/grade 6*
*Wilshire Park Elementary, St. Anthony Village*


TAPESTRY

Your iceberg feelings
can't reach me here.
The wool I wear is warm.
You rattle around in empty rooms,
I waltz in grass-green yarn.
I wove into a tapestry
myself, with colors bright.
My dreams and I are locked away
from your grasping hand.
You search the fabric every day,
but I left no loose threads.

*Billie Ellenson/grade 12*
*St. Francis High School, St. Francis*

## ACROSS THE GALLERY

I am an eagle,
a strong and powerful bird
captured in a painting of winter,
kept in a nest.
Across the hall
is a beautiful painting of spring,
containing a waterfall
in a great evergreen forest.
I wish to be free
to find that spot and soar to it,
unleashing my great strength
to fly again,
float in the cool spring breeze.

*Dan Franz/grade 8*
*Faribault Junior High, Faribault*

i am an eagle

## MY DREAM'S DREAM

What does my dream dream
when I'm asleep?
And what kind of secret
does my dream keep?
Maybe he's dreaming
of being a star,
and having chauffeurs
to drive a new car.
Maybe he's dreaming
of being free,
or maybe he's dreaming
of dreaming with me!

*Julie Munighan/grade 5*
*Sharp Elementary, Moorhead*


My hands are like bushes
I am lost in the world
Sometimes I cry
Sometimes I see fire
My nights are like years
I see red flames in the dark
I have been here for years
I can only see a little light through the bushes
They say I'm a madman but I want peace
I am caged behind bars
I will be set free
I will be lost out there too
But I won't cry in the night
I won't see fire
I'll see gleaming light.

*Tom Crowley/grade 7*
*Monroe Junior High, St. Paul*

My fingers do the walking
    Through the yellowed book pages,
        And over yellowed piano keys,
            Yellow scrambled eggs are picked up,
                And deposited on the fork.

        My fingers do the walking
      Through crisp, crumbly cookie jars,
    And over sloshy milk containers,
  See-through plastic cups are picked up,
And filled with ivory milk.

My fingers do the running
    Through kitchens full of paring knives,
        Gently over sleeping meat cleavers,
           Large and sharp machetes are picked up,
              And deposited far away.

        My fingers do the sleeping,
      After days of work and play,
    Very exhausted after daily dangers,
  But hiding under feather pillows
From dreams of butcher knives.

*Laurence Roberts/grade 7*
*Ramsey Junior High, St. Paul*

## MOUNTAIN VALLEY WALK

A sweet whistle of birds
    keeps my ears in
        solitude.
Fluttering crystals of a
    dainty, mountain stream
        catch my eyes.
A cool calm breath of wind
    gently massages my cheeks.
I come upon a glittering
    pasture.
Gaudy flowers amongst the
    mountain floor.
Birds are drifting
    slowly,
    silently,
forever imprisoning my heart.

*Meredith Hartle/grade 7*
*Owatonna Junior High, Owatonna*

## I WAS WALKING

I was walking through the grass,
I could see off in the field,
Wild horses galloping in the
　　meadow near the house,
Birds flying around in strange
　　formations.
The sky never ends and the
　　wind never stops.

*Brian Johnson/grade 4*
*Thomas Edison Elementary, Moorhead*


## HE WAS THERE

I remember my father,
his eyes beaming brightly as if diamonds,
Someone to stay up and enjoy the late show with,
Someone to play a game of cards with.
When I hit my brother,
He was there to say it was wrong.
Someone who wouldn't tell me
the fur on my coat wasn't real.
He was the one who saved me
From the shadow of the boogie-man.
He was there.

*Burcin Özel/grade 6*
*Indian Mounds Elementary, Bloomington*

CHANGE

An ancient building,
red brick, dingy
with smoke and soot,
the weather of many years.
Curtains hang ragged
in a few grimy windows.
We climb the stone steps,
enter the door
almost rusted open.
Inside the clutter chokes us.
We walk in dimness.
She pulls aside curtains faded,
their green gone or drab.
Sunlight spills in.
She says, "I'll take it."
She, the light she's brought,
already have.

*Carol Kutzer/grade 9*
*Campbell-Tintah High School, Campbell*


TOUCH OF MUSIC

Fingers of flakes
come in a storm of darkness
When I touch the moon
it's now born in echoes
to follow the music
in the woods of dawn

*Marta Parsons/grade 3*
*Maxfield Elementary, St. Paul*

PORTRAIT

My brother is a little raccoon.
His hands reach into everything.
I am the hunter.
I come, I catch him, I aim —
But there's bubble gum stuck in the barrel —
I forgive, and give him a second chance.

*Amy Hauskins/grade 4*
*Elmore Elementary, Elmore*


Friendship is a little old man
carrying around heavy chains
of different sizes, ropes and
other bonds, ready to bind
two people together.
Some he ties with weak bonds
that soon become broken.
Others are bound tightly
with bonds that are broken
only by death.

*Cheryl Chang-Yit/grade 6*
*Probstfield Elementary, Moorhead*

stealing a fish

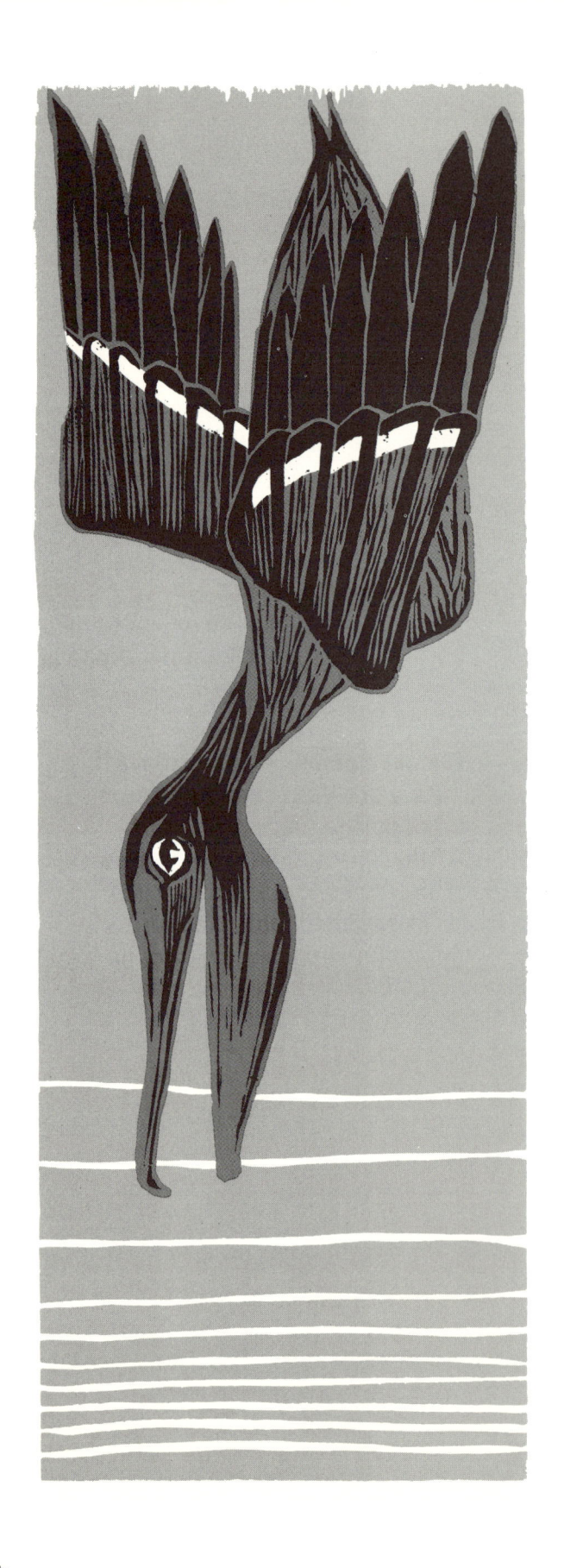

The pelican flaps his wings
over the graceful waves of the ocean.
He hesitates for a moment
then dives in and steals a fish.
The fish struggles for a moment,
but only in vain,
for there is no escaping
to his deep blue home again.

*Brian Lindstrom/grade 8*
*Shakopee Junior High, Shakopee*

LAST WILL AND TESTAMENT

I leave $5,000,000,000,000,000 that you will find
in my Piggy Bank . . . Send it to Heaven
And give my underwear to my sister. Don't forget.
My little ones that have the little cars on them.
And give my leftover sandwich (half eaten) to Sandra, my dog.
I give my bad dream about killer bees to my sister.
And I leave my dream about killing a cat to my dog.
And I leave my dream about killing a mouse to my cat.

I bequeath all my money to be split among
all my relatives.
I leave my pets to my sisters.
I leave my clothes to the poor.
I bequeath my Rolls Royce to my parents.
I leave my mansion to my Cousin Al.
I leave my fleet of ships that cost more than
$1,000,000 to my brother. I leave my money which
even computers can't count to my Uncle Mark. I also
leave South America to my sister.

*Richard Devick/grade 5*
*Our Lady of the Lake School, Mound*


O WHAT A DAY

O what a day, O what a day
My little doggie ran away
I'll wait right here — no more to say
I'm nine years old and turning gray
O what a day, O what a day

*Stephen Hellevik/grade 3*
*Hale School, Minneapolis*

Leap to my arms you green
dog.  Be like your blue ancestors
"the wolves" and be a frog.
Be like your enemy and fall
down.
Be like your father and
kill caribou.  Be like a
shooting star and fly through
the white sky watching the whales
spout up in the night
and the robins will be
flying through
the months and years.

*Jonathan Waugh/grade 5*
*Anwatin Middle School, Minneapolis*


PINBALLS

I'm a Pinball Wizard
I'm shot around
Ring ding
Like a doorbell
As the bells ring
The numbers add up
I go into the drain
I'm shot out again
Ding Ding Ring dong
The numbers add up
Faster and faster
The game is won
And I am pooped
But shot all over again
The Wizard strikes once again

*Dana Oltz/grade 6*
*Rice Elementary, Rice*

WHAT IS NOT:

The tiny pink elephant isn't sailing
  on the dark chocolate river
    that isn't flowing down
      the 100 foot flower that
       isn't dancing in the
        tall green ladies'
         hair that isn't
          walking across
         the still
          purple
        ocean that
       isn't lying flat
     across the big red
    earth that isn't roaming out
   in the big white space that isn't
  sitting on an even bigger planet that
 isn't all green like it's supposed to be and
that isn't flying across the heavens that isn't
standing still.

*Seanne Thomas/grade 7*
*Cleveland Junior High, St. Paul*

he's sinking!

The scents hit you first,
The clean smells of a well-run stable.
The scents of liniment used on stiff horses,
The scent of ammonia used on the floor.
The clean leather, the hay,
Then come the sounds.
You stop to let yourself adjust.
From somewhere across the barn is a radio.
A horse rears up and squeals,
You hear the iron-shod hooves rap the floor.
The intercom comes with a call to the gate.
Hammers of farriers ring through the air.
Concerned voices, all speaking of horses
Circle around in an endless maze.
You see horses and more horses.
Clean limbed show horses bred to perfection.
Being groomed and washed,
Being shoed and tacked
Horses being ridden and watched.
Watched for a wrong move, a mistake
That the judge may pick up.
Yes, all of this hits you when you enter the barn.
But first comes the tension.
The air almost pings with the tension.
The tension that comes before a performance.
A performance of any kind.
The horses feel it.
The owners feel it.
You, an outsider, are held in awe
Of the tension,
Of the awareness,
Of the barns on a show day.

*Maryellen Minogue/grade 8*
*Central Junior High, Columbia Heights*

## DIFFERENT STROKES

Whistling a catchy tune the woman
stepped out onto the curb
A nearby priest drank a Coca-Cola
while he kicked a rock steadily along

Up the block an accountant paints
his home
down the alley the housewife mails
her bills

From a distance the old steeple can
be seen
To the right the new one being built
To the left the president of Univac
rides his bicycle to his office

On the outskirts of town lies
the old dump
where ancient memorable cars
lie shamefully apart
the factories are boiling, the hot
stoves are cooking
When the children are starving why
won't we listen?

The duck which just died
flutters along
the gun which just shot it must
be cleaned and polished
and taken home

*Tom Garton/grade 12*
*Lincoln Senior High, Bloomington*

They paint big eyes on me
but I do not see.
They paint ears on me
but I do not hear.
They didn't paint a heart on me,
but inside I still feel.
They pull my strings
and make me move,
They pull more
and make me smile,
inside I still feel hurt.
They cannot paint tears
but I still cry.

*Patty Polensky/grade 7*
*Perham High School, Perham*


MUSIC BOX

I feel like a dancer
in a music box.
In the morning I'm wound up
and all ready to go.
I do the same thing
over and over
but before I finish
I'm tired and my box
is closed.

It hurts being on
my tippy toes all day.
I don't really like to dance,
but I have to.
I want to sing . . . but
someone else does it for me.

*Jan Pioske/grade 10*
*Le Sueur High School, Le Sueur*

A broken heart that crashes
like glass that falls to the floor.
There was so much pain from the cut
that didn't even show.
The scar was left from the hurt
inside my heart.
You're so far away
and still you grab me
in the dark.

*Sylvia Tyler/age 15*
*Booth-Brown House, St. Paul*


STARS

They give light
for the moon to see
as they flash
across the Milky Way
and pour themselves
on the world below,
flying across the sky
like angels of light.

*Denise Bissener/grade 6*
*Jordan Elementary, Jordan*

no way!

## IF TREES TOOK OVER THIS WORLD

The world was taken over by trees. They would put you to work. Here's what people would be doing: Washing their leaves, combing their bark, digging up good soil, watering their soil.

Laws would be: No cutting down trees. No lumber jacks. People would have to sit outside in snow and rain. The trees would sit in houses under a special light. The punishments would be: No soil for a week or no water. The stores would be larger so the trees could fit. They would sell soil, water, and little trees. It would be different. Would you like it? I wouldn't. No way no tree is going to take over this world.

*Daniel Clemmensen/grade 5*
*Washington Elementary, Faribault*

If caterpillars were trains
then butterflies would be planes.

If cats turned into fog
it would creep silently up
and silently away.

If the world was made of candy
then everyone would have a sweet life.

*Kris Holstad/grade 5*
*John F. Kennedy Elementary, Lakeville*


My poem starts out on a light purple rainy day.
I saw a man sitting under a tree in the middle
   of a pasture.
He can see a dandelion, far in the distance, and
   a lamb sitting near it.
The man began to think: We, the dandelion, lamb and
   myself have something in common.
We are alone. I will sing a song about all of us.
And then I will meet them one by one.
And we will then be together, on this lonely day.

*Venisa Dinius/grade 8*
*St. Margaret Mary School, Golden Valley*

Do you know who I am?
A reader of the sky. Yes.
A goddess? No.
I am so young I could not
hold No to myself anymore.
My eyes could never see
the purple moon in the sky.
I forgot how happy I was
before I was dead.

*Terri Anderson/grade 5*
*Park Elementary, Le Sueur*


In my dreaming mind,
waves are swirling
stones into a big rainbow
leaves the earth covering
a whole bunch of stars
and bring the moon
over like a magnet
and pulling it under
the rainbow
and making a movie
of this poem lighting the sky.

*Tony Killian/grade 3*
*Highland Park Elementary, St. Paul*

## SHELTER FROM THE NIGHT

The sun shines powerful
Conquering the dark
Fighting for its goal
The moon is weak
Doesn't overpower the world
For it gives up and doesn't try
But they both serve a purpose
To take up the empty sky
To make us feel content
That we are not left out.

*Maureen Drobac/grade 11*
*Agape School, St. Paul*


## AN OLD BOOK

Surrounded by pillows lying half dead.
I look into my book, which is opened like
The palm of a child's hand asking for candy.
The book is full of old-fashioned Saturday
Excitement, no school and no work to be
Nailed down to.
I hold its thin feather-like pages in
My hot sweaty hand — eagerly trying to
Be done first.
Some day I may live the life of the
Book in an old-fashioned Saturday way.

*Patty Asmus/grade 6*
*Blue Earth Elementary, Blue Earth*

## SUNFLOWER (VIET NAM MEMORY)

I feel the wind through my face
and dripping water on my head.
But I never can see what is around me,
or ahead of me, there is always
a thick green wall covering
my bright yellow eye.
It seems like I stand alone
in the middle of nowhere.
Now I can feel a great wind come again.
It comes to my green body
like shooting bullets.
My back bends down after the wind has gone.
My eye touches the cooling ground.
I struggle, but then give out.
Now no one will know I was here,
except the mighty winds.

*Quyen Huynh/grade 9*
*Blue Earth High School, Blue Earth*

FEELINGS

I heard a song that opened my heart
and moonlight flowed within me
I tried to go with it, to enter
my secret dreams
With joy I flew into the distance,
and a thread of light seemed to bring
me toward itself.
And then my joy turned to anger
And I dropped like a stone into the
darkness.

*Matt Feeney/grade 5*
*Highland Park Elementary, St. Paul*

dropped like a stone

## THE SORRY MASK SLIPS

She yelled at me for not hanging my clothes on the line.
I put on the mask that shows how sorry I am.
On she went, her thundering voice
towering over me like a black cloud.
My sorry mask worked very well for awhile,
but, seeing the load of clothes snapping in the wind
must have ripped the seams:
My mask shattered and I broke out laughing.

*April Tousignant/grade 8*
*Milaca Middle School/Milaca*


Hot, dry eyed
I grab my coat and slam the door.
Dusk around me, nearly night.
I look at the bare trees
silhouetted against the sky.
Dry leaves scurry around my feet
as if in a frenzy to get nowhere —
sort of like me.

*Andrea McAllister/grade 12*
*Battle Lake High School, Battle Lake*

It's Saturday night, restless
like a shaky spoonful of jelly.
I wish for wings to set me on
flight to some place of pink, hazy
lace and soda fizz.
It seems such a waste to be
stuck in this hive-home, like a blob
of honey deposited by indifferent
bees.

*Melanie Hamilton/grade 9*
*Apollo High School, St. Cloud*


THE THINGS

I fear the things.
Dark and Damp & alone.
The big place is filled with
space. Lots of space I can't
see. But I can hear the space.
The things move & watch & wait.
When will they come out?
I sit in Dad's chair. Where they
can't hurt me — I close my eyes so
they can't see me.

*Dave Berger/grade 11*
*Onamia High School, Onamia*

As I approach the old hill
I look around and hear the birds.
I hear animals whispering to me.
The wind whistles through the
branches. I sit on an old log
to rest. The night comes.
I sit still, until I disappear
into the stars.

*Margarita Castanon/grade 5*
*Sabin Elementary, Moorhead*

Loosen your hands in sleep.
Loosen your dreams in twilight.
Take the pattern of night
and sleep easy.

Gather the stars turning in the wind.
Gather the faces of the happy ones.
Sing in the night against the wind,
Float along the beautiful sky
and sleep easy.

Dream of the dreams that never were.
Dream of the dreams that never will.
Dream of the gypsy dancing in the night,
Dream of my hands ending the years
and sleep easy.

*Kathy Erb/grade 8*
*St. Mark's School, St. Paul*

baboons

In my friend's house I'll never see baboons on the green
hanging lamp. I will never see sun in the kitchen.
I will never hear the sounds of the ocean,
or even touch the ocean for that matter.
Nor the sweet smell of the calendar roasting over the hot stove.
I won't be able to see
or do anything in the jungle of South America . . . in my friend's house.
In his house, I won't find a big, big hole.
I'd first find a television set with my favorite show on it.
A deck of cards just waiting to be played.

*Terry Fergen/grade 6*
*Thomas Edison Elementary, Moorhead*

## SOUNDS OF DREAMING

I was in my silent house,
My cat was as soft as a fur coat
hanging in the closet,
The couch was as shy as a stranger
walking by,
The rug was so still I thought
it was dreaming.

The chair was peaceful and she thought
it was a statue.
The door was whispering to the T.V.
so quietly she thought they were
daydreaming.

The spices on the shelf were
thinking of peaceful dreams.
The car was telling secrets to the
garage as silently as motionless
strangers.

She thought the tables had withdrawn
because they were so quiet,
The spider crawling on the wall
was as silent as a dream.
She whispered to her cat very softly,
"I love you," and very peacefully
went to bed.
And then, the whole house went
drowsily to sleep.

*Wendie Paulsen/grade 5*
*Phalen Lake Elementary, St. Paul*

NIGHTTIME DREAMS

At midnight the old men remain
Alone with their bitter thoughts
And dark and dusky reminiscences
They become young again,
They relive their life,
From playgrounds to law school
They don't talk
Their minds are too busy to speak
Their subconscious takes over
For the night

They become alive wearing color-
Ful clothes, holding the world
In their hands
But the world falls apart
Dark clouds storm in their minds
The storm tears their minds
They leave their bodies to wander,
And have not others who feel happy
They find people who are worse
Than they
Who are troubled over doing
Simple chores
They are ashamed
They return back to their bodies
And awake to start another day

*Bob Votel/grade 8*
*Providence Schools of St. John Vianney,*
*South St. Paul*

THE NOBODY MAN

If he was a journey, I would try to talk to him, but he was like a
detour. He would take the bridge over his and my problems and say, "I am the
wrong way." I always felt blocked off from him as if there was a DO NOT
         ENTER
sign ten feet in front of him. It was like a stop light that flashed red and
green. You could come close if it was green. There were no rest stops, just
a journey for him. But there were so many ruts and pot holes. His darkness
         and
emptiness were like a long lonely dirt road, like no exit, no shoulder and no
         place
to stop. But I always saw the DO NOT PASS sign in his eyes and his only
         turn off.

*anonymous/age 16*
*Arlington House School, St. Paul*

It so happens I am sick of being
16 years old.

I can't go to R rated movies
Can't get good jobs
I have to obey my parents
I have a curfew
Can't always do what I want
I have to go to school
Can't become a U.S. Senator
Can't write good poems
My feet are too big
I can't write neatly
I can't

*Chris James/grade 11*
*Mariner Senior High, White Bear Lake*


I am the dancer
who moves according
to the music I hear.

You are the music.

Many times I could hear love
and happiness in your music —
one time I thought I heard a promise,
but that was only an illusion because
I was lost in your melody and forgot
to listen to the harmony.

I was a dancer and you
were the music I danced to.

I am still a dancer
but with different music —
Now I am much more careful
to listen to the harmony.

*Lisa Tenny/grade 12*
*St. James Senior High, St. James*

the black river

THE BLACK RIVER

The black river rages endlessly on.
Over the stones, sucking at stray branches,
Pulling them down its gloomy depths.
It rushes down a valley where horses quench their thirst.
The moon is covered by clouds, and a single star shines.
The face of a mountain steadily stares into the river.
A small tree, uprooted and thrown into the river
Floats on, and a small ant confusedly walks down its bark.
As the river runs over the rocks it flattens out the reeds.
The reeds bow toward the road as the river hurries on.
As a peddler stoops to drink, his rags are sucked into the river,
He cries out in agony, and throws himself in after them.
The next morning a traveler finds his bones.

*Robin Krueger/grade 6*
*Beacon Heights Elementary, Plymouth*

The storm moved like a blazing ship
ready to explode.
It has traveled the snowy beds of darkness.
It came from the gold ships floating
away into the storm.
It sounded like the new dream of earth
ready to explode from the sleepy coldness.
The snow will swoop out of the clouds
dropping its new white wings.
The secret is that the blind hawks are
beaming toward us with grassy wings.

*Nicole Mannarino/grade 3*
*Maxfield Elementary, St. Paul*

THE SEA

I looked at the sky
and then at water.
As the waves rolled in
the clouds moved out in a secret
but joyful silver.
The flow of the sea
rushed in on me
and all I saw was shining black.
As I lifted my head out of the water
a wave crashed over my head
as an explosion of white petals.

*Chuck Fowler/grade 6*
*Edward Neill Elementary, Robbinsdale*

I dream of climbing the golden ladder
swimming with shadows
in a house of gold.
In my dreams the shapes of clouds
begin with mountains.
In my dreams everybody is lost among sunlight.
In my dreams windows lead to butterflies.
There are post offices for animals.
I search for mist of different colors.
In my dreams people hold handfuls of fire.
It seems that everything is scattering through space.

*Amy Helin/grade 3*
*Champlin Elementary, Champlin*

windows lead to butterflies

## FRIENDS

If you were leaving I would give you
my eyes like little flashlights.
I would give you a black witch's ear that would
do magic! I would give you shoes
that would show you around.
I would give you my soul for a friend.

*Debra Burke/grade 3*
*Dowling School, Minneapolis*


## HOSPITAL SILENCE

Sitting alone in a hospital bed
at night. Looking around the room
seeing nothing but darkness.
All I hear is a padded beat of
people walking down the hall.
It sounds like a drum beating
softly in the mist.
I feel like I'm in a dark quiet
old house looking for a light,
seeing my family just
out of reach.

*Rebecca Kay Kurtzahn/grade 5*
*Pilgrim Lane Elementary, Plymouth*

QUIET . . .

It's as
quiet as inside
our heads or like a
bottle of ketchup sit-
ting in the refrigerator.
When I'm home alone   read-
ing a book all I can hear
is the dog's chain clink-
ing together while she
walks, the sink going
drip, drop because
someone forgot to
turn it off.  Or
quiet as an ear-
ring on some-
one's ear.

*Debbie Brewer/grade 5*
*Immaculate Heart of Mary School, Minnetonka*

COWBOY HERO

I will write about you,
With long sentences
Your mustang is strong
The ranch is musty
I will write about your family
In my story will be
Your friends
For they helped you grow
They are like the rocks in an avalanche.

*Katie Corson/grade 6*
*Hillcrest Elementary, Bloomington*



Hey crater face!
  What are you
    holding in your basket?

Tucked in the
  corner is the lunar loaf
    fresh from the stars.

Covered in the glass
laps in the ocean waves.

For dessert
  you pick the apple
    from the sky
and earth rolls about
    your finger by the stem.

Relish
  in the
    kiss of the sun.

*Kari Snow/grade 11*
*Mariner Senior High, White Bear Lake*

At dawn the seagulls come to the boats, their stomachs empty and their beaks open. The gulls are fishermen, they are going to sea, going to catch the fish. They don't look back at the beach, they keep on going out to sea.

The town is hungry again, and the people are afraid, the seagulls know it. The fish in the sea are happy, they are warm and comfortable, but they are only fish.

The clouds pass over the cold dark water and the captain starts the old steam engine. The old seamen appear upon the deck, checking their nets and trimming the ropes.

At the stern the captain stands writing in his log and looking towards the rising sun. He turns around and finishes his entry into the log, slamming the book shut and hiding it away. He knows his men don't trust him.

*Steve Krekelberg/grade 8*
*Southwest High School, Minneapolis*

LUTEFISK

They haul me out of the water like
a man being taken to prison.  They grab
me to take a hook out of my mouth.  I look
back one last time to my home and see
my mother and father crying.  I am in a
boat with my other fish being taken to Norway
for selling.  I feel a knife running down my
spine searching for meat.  I find myself
in an opening inside a person.  I feel like
someone who got lost in a store whose mother
left for home.  I am all alone now in this
big opening all alone
by myself, all alone . . .

*Terry Nokken/grade 6*
*Riverside Elementary, Moorhead*

THE FINGERS

"Ladies and gentlemen, it's an
honor to present to you, the
fingers . . ."
"Thank you, thank you — notice
the accuracy of the knuckles'
position under the soft, and
silky skin, the extraordinary
smoothness of the fingernails,
and the roaming movement of the
fabulous, exhilarating fingers
themselves.
I have a complaint here concerning the W.W.F.A. — World Wide Finger Association . . . Watch where
you put those babies."
"Ladies and gentlemen, the fingers!"

*Mary Keating/grade 5*
*Washington Elementary, Faribault*

five fish climbing mount everest

THE BRAVE FISH

A living fish is camping in the desert.
He is well equipped. There is a safari
of fish following him. He is eating at
tables of nothing. He will never become
famous as a fish and will never get large
rewards. Only shall he get fame if he goes
on alone. Only once before has a fish
expedition been so dangerous, that's when
5 fish climbed Mount Everest.

*Kevin Ryan/grade 5*
*Probstfield Elementary, Moorhead*

Fear is like green and yellow seaweed
around the shore.
The squeak of the dry hinges sings
a song called fright.
Meanwhile the shriveling
olives let off a pimento scent.
The black cat cowardly awaits in
the dark corner.

*Sheryl Pittelkow/grade 11*
*South High School, Minneapolis*


In the stillness of the quiet boxcar, dark and quiet,
and the sway of the wind as it blows.
Well, you faint away in the boxcar when it sways
on the tracks as the moon shall shine to the wind.
The covers over your head and the stillness of your
bedroom as you go into dream land and you shall dream
away into your class and you hear the sheets say hello
to the wall and the stillness of your bedroom surrounds
you.

*Scott Halverson/grade 3*
*J.J. Hill Elementary, St. Paul*

I am on top of the sun when it rises.
I am the pole that holds the tent.
When I die, the rooster will not crow at dawn,
the crickets will not chirp at night and
the leaves will not return in the spring.
I remember crying in my room at night,
missing my freedom.
I remember holding my puppy, wiping
her wet kisses from my face.
I am the moss in the thick of the woods.
I am in the track, guiding the train.

*Cathy Steblay/grade 12*
*Orono High School, Long Lake*


Hope is the thing with feathers
Like birds soaring in the sky.
Trusting their feathers,
Hoping to be on time to the South Pole.

There was a man with a tongue of wood.
His wife had a heart of stone.
She had given him the tongue of wood,
So he couldn't speak for himself.

Everybody knows things —
The laws of nature,
Like the bird who sings,
And the birds who don't.

*Carol Hagen/grade 6*
*Randolph Heights Elementary, St. Paul*

clouds are marshmallows
they float and melt in your mouth
soft cushions of foam

*Mari Peterson/grade 6*
*Cokato Elementary, Cokato*

eyeglasses are cool
they always will show the way
they will never cry

*Barb Hannus/grade 5*
*Dassel Elementary, Dassel*

CAMPING OUT IN THE FOREST

When I'm out camping
    in the forest in the night
        it's so quiet you can hear
            the animals talking to each other.
                You can hear the owls hooting.
                    It almost sounds like a
masquerade party and everyone is having
    a good time, and the leaves and the wind,
        the wind makes the leaves shake and it sounds
           like chains rattling and I can see the fire
               blazing with rage like it's mad and the sparks
                  flying and the fire crackling like a mountain
                      when it starts to crack and fall.  It sounds
like an avalanche and all these sounds
    are sounds from the forest at night.

*Ranae Palmer/grade 5*
*Georgetown Elementary, Georgetown*

The feather has a color that
Looks like shadows. People dancing,
Moving in and around dark curtains.
Drums beating a long time ago in
A small village. Strobing lights and
Prancing feet in harmony with nature.
Pet pheasants come to listen and spread
Their wings with delight. A small eager
Boy comes and chases the pheasants;
With surprise gets a feather. He sees
The dancing of his people in the feather.

*Jeanne Van Lith/grade 12*
*Monticello High School, Monticello*

the dancing of his people

I'm up in the attic,
behind an old bike and a rocking chair.
Mice, crickets and spiders are crawling on me.

They don't care.
The windows are covered with faded cloth.
Little light is coming through.
Once in awhile things get piled on me.
I get pushed back farther and farther.
My paint is chipped, all the varnish is gone.
I bet they don't even know I'm here.
But if they did, they wouldn't care.

*Melissa Preiner/grade 6*
*Poplar Bridge Elementary, Bloomington*


I NEED

a forest of willow trees in
    spring
with lilacs in bloom at its
    edges
moss grows thick on once
    worn paths
and ferns grow along their
    edges
and
dresses of long ago when
    Conestoga wagons
        rocked over rough trails
            heading west

bonnets little girls wear as
    they gather water from
        nearby creeks.

*Valerie Tollefson/grade 11*
*Crookston Senior High, Crookston*

## A COCONUT

I seem to be a coconut
Falling on someone's head.
But really I am a nut being cracked.

I seem to be a dog barking,
Barking its head off.
But really I am a cat running away.

I seem to be a spider.
Dangling in a web.
But really I am a fly in a spider's web,
Knowing it's the END.

*Joe Stone/grade 4*
*Carmon Elementary, Faribault*


## STUPIDITY

Stupidity is two people. One is wearing
old ragged tennis shoes, pants with holes,
and a T-shirt. The other is in a new pair
of double-knit pants, a bow-tie, glasses,
a nicely knit sweater, two-tone shoes,
and a top hat. The messy one recites a
complex mathematical equation while the
other thinks 7+ 4= 18. The clean person
(let's call him Lou) and the messy one
(let's call him Louis the Third) are really
the same people. They are in all of us.
One appears on our surface at a time, each
one trying to destroy the other in a
constant battle which sometimes leads to
insanity.

*Nick Christenson/grade 5*
*Riverside Elementary, Moorhead*

## I'VE COME TO THE CONCLUSION

I've come to the conclusion,
Now I've come to know,
You can not build a snowman,
If you haven't any snow.

*Jessica Lorentz/grade 4*
*Cannon Falls Elementary, Cannon Falls*


## WHAT IT IS TO BE MONEY

Some days crumpled up in billfolds.
Sometimes locked inside cash registers.
Now and then people try to steal me.
Most don't but some do.
In a few years I'll probably be
shredded for insulation.
Then I'll be stuffed in some building
to rot away forever.

*Tim Golly/grade 5*
*Winnebago Elementary, Winnebago*

DID YOU KNOW AN ONION HAS A LIFE OF ITS OWN?

The onion is like the inner bark of a tree. It has two eyes which show its age by all the wrinkles they have. It sounds like a mild bowl of rice crispies. The onion is protected by two thin layers of skin to keep the strong odor in.
The onion is packed together like the streets of New York on rush hour. Throughout the 15 pieces of the onion each and every one has its own shape, each fitting in.
Stacked together it looks like a lady in the old western days with a hoop skirt and a hat with a flower coming out.
Inside the onion is a war between two groups of people seeing which could put out the most odor.

*Brian Pass/grade 9*
*Worthington Junior High, Worthington*

I'm not a wound full of hurt,
or tube full of First Aid Cream,
but I'm a white bandage
wrapped . . .
a little white scheme.

*Kerrie O'Connor/grade 9*
*Monroe Junior High, St. Paul*


I'm tired of Abraham Lincoln
staring at me with copper eyes.
I'm tired of realists telling me
people don't fly.
(I'm certain they've never tried.)
I'm tired of 2+2=4 and
all the rest.
Some wonderful person has told me
that 2+2=4
for some reason that
I don't understand, (or believe.)
I'm tired of eyelashes
(they make me nervous)
mostly though I'm tired of
waking up in the middle of my
Shark dream.
I may never die.
Won't someone find me a tin penny?

*Terri Wisdorf/grade 12*
*Hastings High School, Hastings*

There was a little kitten up in a maple tree she found a little hole and found it was empty so she thought it couldn't be a maple tree but it was so she went to get some maple syrup to fill the tree so no one would be disappointed when they came for maple syrup

*Julie Savat/grade 6*
*George Washington Elementary, Moorhead*

The stars shine like gold in the sky,
The sky like a blue ocean.
I want to be part of it,
But my body is stealing me away.
I can hear the wind's voice,
It is singing me a song.
I want to be part of it,
But my body is stealing me away.
I can feel the children as they play,
Cries, laughter, voices,
I want to be part of it,
But my body is stealing me away.

*Lara Etnier/grade 3*
*Glen Lake Elementary, Hopkins*

## THE JOURNEYS OF SUMMER

How far do we stretch before the sun
cracks into our hearts?
setting us ablaze
crackling
blinding
until we cannot even look at ourselves
for the pain and fear of it
floating on a dream
into your smile
tossing and turning in the valleys
of your breath
drifting into the chambers of your fantasies
lost in the darkness of your wishes
I can smell
the faces sizzling on the July sidewalk
flowing into each other
blending the happiness with the dread
crisp on the edges, scorched in the center
their laughter boils into tears
washing them away to the sea.
The sea, who is the keeper of apple cores
holder of watermelon rinds, of eggshells and
half eaten corn muffins
streamlined from garbage disposals somewhere
in New York City
a bird watches the fading feathers of the
sunset
and wades in the twilight
to the edge of a melting globe.
He is trained to follow the faintest whisper
from the hidden corners
of my special self

*Cathy Bryan/grade 12*
*Sibley High School, West St. Paul*

Flame you are glorious like nothing
I've seen you're powerful but sometimes
so small you glow in the dark
so pretty and Bright you're in me
and out of me at the same time
so bright I adore you i truly adore
you o I do I do you flow in my
mind little flame yes you do
like silk you flow in my mind
like a Blade in Butter yes you do
you do

*Shawn Wadleigh/grade 4*
*John F. Kennedy Elementary, Hastings*

The star spins gently,
lonely, cut off from brothers
by the endless void.

The aging comet
wants to rest, tired
of searching emptiness.

Blinded by their lights
the comet, star converge.
Suddenly, such brilliance!

*Walter Stumpf/grade 10*
*Richfield Senior High, Richfield*

The green meadow with the
green leaves on the trees blowing
swiftly. The bark as rough
as jagged rocks.

The river flowing swiftly
so blue as the sky.

A single robin
is watching.
A single robin
is singing.

*Darcy Running/grade 6*
*Savage Elementary, Savage*

a single robin is watching

# Index

of the schools and writers who participated in the 78-79 program:

Agape School, St. Paul/poet, Deborah Keenan
Anwatin Middle School, Minneapolis/poet, John Minczeski
Apollo High School, St. Cloud/poet, Margaret Hasse
Arlington House School, St. Paul/poet, Kate Green
Battle Lake High School, Battle Lake/poet, John Caddy
Beacon Heights Elementary, Plymouth/poet, John Engman
Blue Earth Elementary, Blue Earth/poet, Margaret Hasse
Blue Earth High School, Blue Earth/poet, John Caddy
Booth-Brown House, St. Paul/poet, Kate Green
Campbell-Tintah High School, Campbell/poet, Caroline Marshall
Cannon Falls Elementary, Cannon Falls/poet, Keith Harrison
Central Junior High, Columbia Heights/poet, John Rezmerski
Champlin Elementary, Champlin/poet, Ruth Roston
Cleveland Junior High, St. Paul/poet, Kate Green
Community Education Services: Garlough Elementary and
    Sibley High School, West St. Paul/poet, Alvaro Cardona-Hine
Crookston Public Schools, Crookston/poet, Marisha Chamberlain
    /poet, Cary Waterman
Dassel-Cokato Public Schools, Dassel and Cokato
    /poet, Alvaro Cardona-Hine
Edina-East Senior High, Edina/poet, Keith Harrison
Edward Neill Elementary, Robbinsdale/poet, Kate Green
Elmore Elementary, Elmore/poet, John Caddy
Faribault Junior High, Faribault/poet, John Caddy
George Washington Elementary, Moorhead/poet, Alvaro Cardona-Hine
Georgetown Elementary, Moorhead/poet, Cary Waterman
Glen Lake Elementary, Hopkins/poet, Deborah Keenan
Glencoe High School, Glencoe/poet, Cary Waterman
Hale School and Dowling School, Minneapolis/poet, Mary Logue
Hastings Senior High, Hastings/poet, Mary Karr
Hiawatha Elementary, Minneapolis/poet, Marisha Chamberlain
Highland Park Elementary, St. Paul/poet, Kate Green
Hillcrest Elementary, Bloomington/poet, Mary Logue
Immaculate Heart of Mary School, Minnetonka/poet, Cary Waterman
Indian Mounds Elementary, Bloomington/poet, John Caddy
J.J. Hill Elementary, St. Paul/poet, Deborah Keenan
Jefferson Elementary, South St. Paul/poet, Alvaro Cardona-Hine
John F. Kennedy Elementary, Hastings/poet, Michael Dennis Browne
John F. Kennedy Elementary, Lakeville/poet, Alvaro Cardona-Hine
Jordan Elementary, Jordan/poet, Kate Green
Le Sueur High School, Le Sueur/poet, Cary Waterman
Lincoln Elementary, Moorhead/poet, Caroline Marshall
Lincoln Senior High, Bloomington/poet, Alvaro Cardona-Hine
Mariner Senior High, White Bear Lake/poet, Alvaro Cardona-Hine
    /poet, Marisha Chamberlain
    /poet, Candyce Clayton
    /poet, George Roberts

Maxfield Elementary, St. Paul/poet, Kate Green
Milaca Middle School, Milaca/poet, John Caddy
Monroe Junior High, St. Paul/poet, Deborah Keenan
Monticello High School, Monticello/poet, William Meissner
Murray Junior-Senior High, St. Paul/poet, Deborah Keenan
North Branch Middle School, North Branch/poet, Mary Logue
Onamia High School, Onamia/poet, Cary Waterman
Orchard Lake Elementary, Lakeville/poet, Dana Christian Jensen
Orono High School, Long Lake/poet, Mary Karr
Our Lady of the Lake School, Mound/poet, Dana Christian Jensen
Owatonna Junior High, Owatonna/poet, Dana Christian Jensen
Park Elementary, Le Sueur/poet, Dana Christian Jensen
Perham High School, Perham/poet, John Caddy
Phalen Lake Elementary, St. Paul/poet, Deborah Keenan
Pilgrim Lane School, Plymouth/poet Cary Waterman
Poplar Bridge Elementary, Bloomington/poet, John Caddy
Probstfield Elementary, Moorhead/poet, Mary Logue
/poet, Mark Vinz
Providence School of St. John Vianney, South St. Paul/poet, John Engman
Ramsey Junior High, St. Paul/poet, Deborah Keenan
Randolph Heights Elementary, St. Paul/poet, Deborah Keenan
Rice Elementary, Rice/poet, John Rezmerski
Richfield Senior High, Richfield/poet, John Caddy
/poet, Caroline Marshall
Riverside Elementary, Moorhead/poet, Caroline Marshall
/poet, John Minczeski
Roosevelt Elementary, St. Paul/poet, Kate Green
Sabin Elementary, Moorhead/poet, Mark Vinz
St. Francis High School, St. Francis/poet, John Caddy
St. James Senior High, St. James/poet, John Caddy
St. Margaret Mary School, Golden Valley/poet, John Engman
St. Mark's School, St. Paul/poet, Deborah Keenan
Savage Elementary, Savage/poet, Deborah Keenan
Shakopee Junior High, Shakopee/poet, Alvaro Cardona-Hine
Sharp Elementary, Moorhead/poet, Mark Vinz
South High School, Minneapolis/poet, Mary Logue
Southwest High School, Minneapolis/poet, John Engman
/poet, Mary Logue
Thomas Edison Elementary, Moorhead/poet, Jim Fawbush
/poet, Mary Karr
Washburn Elementary, Bloomington/poet, Ruth Roston
Washington, Carmon, and Nerstrand Elementary Schools, Faribault
/poet, Marisha Chamberlain
Wilshire Park and Silver Oak Elementary Schools, St. Anthony Village
/poet, Ruth Roston
Winnebago Elementary, Winnebago/poet, Keith Harrison
Worthington Junior High, Worthington/poet, Bill Holm

# Editor
# Mark Vinz

Mark Vinz has been a member of Minnesota Poets in the Schools since 1974, and he also works in the North Dakota program. His poems have appeared in over 90 magazines and anthologies, and in six chapbook collections, the most recent of which are *Contingency Plans* (published as a part of the Autumn 1978 *Ohio Review*) and *Deep Water, Dakota* (Juniper Press). He teaches at Moorhead State University, edits the poetry journal *Dacotah Territory*, and lives with his wife, Betsy, and daughters, Katie (age 10) and Sarah (age 8).

# Illustrator
# Gaylord Schanilec

Gaylord Schanilec's heart is hidden under a bridge in the Red River Valley of North Dakota. He has illustrated a number of small press books of poetry, most recently *Shemuel*, by Rochelle Owens, (New Rivers Press). His own poems have appeared in *The Mainstreeter* and *North Country*.

NORMANDALE COMMUNITY COLLEGE
LIBRARY
9700 FRANCE AVENUE SOUTH
BLOOMINGTON MN 55431-4399